ELSEWHEREVILLE

By Melanie J. Vogel

Illustrated by Carey Lancaster

Melanie J. Vogel Publishing www.melaniejvogel.com

ISBN: 978-1-7330199-3-4

DEDICATIONS

To my daughter, Millena who has always had the courage to do her own thing.

And to all the kids who fit out much better than they fit in.

Melanie

To all the children of the world, young and old. Let your light shine and embrace who you are!

To my daughter, Izzy and in memory of my niece, Xandra. I love you, forever and always.

Carey

CONTENTS

CHAPTER ONE: KISS THE BUG!

Tuesday, ten minutes before all the magic happens.

"Hey, freak show, you gonna kiss that bug you're talking to?"

I look up. Ugh! It's Sierra Simpkins, half of the duo who's come to be known as the bane of my fifth-grade life.

"Everybody come see this!" Sierra sneers. "Myrtle Hitchabocker's gonna lock lips with a wooly worm."

All the fifth graders on the playground turn and stare at me.

"That's ridiculous!" I say, "Because worms don't have lips, and this particular little guy is the caterpillar form of an Isabella Tiger Moth. So, you see, he's really not a worm at all."

"You're a freak, Myrtle Hitchabocker. You're different, and your head's in the clouds. You wear weirdo clothes, and you have a weirdo name. You're not like us, freak. You'll never fit in!"

Sierra bends down to where I'm sitting in the grass at the edge of the playground.

"You," she pokes her finger into my sweater vest, purposely avoiding an old grape jelly stain, "are the biggest weirdo at Parkside Intermediate School. You're not the same as us and you'll never fit in. Now kiss the bug!"

Sebrina, Sierra's much larger twin sister, laughs a big, snorty snort. All the other fifth graders circle around us, and a goofy cheer breaks out in the crowd. "Kiss the bug, Myrtle! Kiss the bug!" *Clap, clap.* "Kiss the bug, Myrtle! Kiss the bug!" *Clap, clap.* Then the cheer turns into a chant. "Kiss it! Kiss it! Kiss it! Kiss it!"

Sebrina reaches out her huge hand at me and

squishes up my cheeks into a kissy fish face. Her deep lumberjack/linebacker/lady wrestler-voice booms, "Pucker up, worm-lover."

Of course, at that moment, a girl in the back of the crowd has to snap a picture of me on her phone. I bet she's writing *Loser!* for the caption.

Sierra picks up the caterpillar, and it curls into a ball in her hand. She shoves it against my lips. She makes a minute-long exaggerated kissing sound with her mouth. After that, Sebrina lets go of my face.

"That's better!" Sierra pushes me back. She holds the caterpillar up to her own face now.

"Hello there, little buddy," she says in a sappy-sounding voice, pretending to be me. "I'm so glad you are my little friend, worm. I'm so weird and strange that nobody else in a billion-trillion years would want to be my friend."

She sticks her tongue out at me and puts the caterpillar back in the grass next to me. Then Sebrina raises her gigantic foot above the caterpillar and smashes the little bug with her size eleven women's shoe, smearing the caterpillar into the ground. Pulverized.

CHAPTER TWO: DIFFERENT

Okay. I'm different from all the other fifth graders at Parkside Intermediate. I get that. But it seems to me that no matter what I do or wherever I go, someone is always pointing that out. I just don't fit in.

I talk to bugs and flowers. They never talk back, but I guess I just need an animal or plant who will listen, really. I guess that makes me a freak. And I like to think about stuff kids my age don't normally think about. Like, how big is Big Foot's foot? How do we know dinosaurs roared? What if they just clucked like chickens?

To make things worse, my family doesn't have much money. My dad got really sick last year and lost his job because he missed so much work. Mom tried to pick up the slack by selling mattresses on commission, but so far, she's only sold one. And that was to my grandma. I have to wear clothes that other fifth graders don't wear, hand-me-downs from my older cousin Ethyl Mae.

For whatever reason, Ethyl Mae has a big thing for Bermuda shorts, striped sweater vests, and those fuzzy knee socks that remind you of small animals crawling up legs. Ethyl Mae always manages to smudge all her sweater vests with either spaghetti sauce or grape jelly before gifting them to me.

When Sierra and Sebrina and the other fifth graders get to wear new jeans or cute skirts to school, I must wear my hand-me-down Bermuda shorts and stained striped sweater vests.

On school pride day, when every other kid wore our school colors, I made the glorious 'fashion faux pas' of wearing green and black polka dots with purple pinstripes. I can't always figure that fashion stuff out on my own, you know. I don't mean to be different. I just am.

At recess, when all the other kids play kickball or swing on swings, I usually sit on the edge of the playground where the grass starts to grow and smell the tiny purple violets that bloom there. It's a nice place. Sometimes I talk to insects or count clouds.

Those stupid Simpkins Sisters laugh at me and say things like, "Myrtle Hitchabocker, you're a freak show!"

Sierra has a high-pitched giggle that screeches like a chipmunk chattering, and Sebrina snorts a low, snorty grunt that sounds like a pig digging around in the mud for truffles.

They make such ugly faces that sometimes I wonder if they might someday get stuck like that. And I secretly hope that they do.

CHAPTER THREE: FIT IN

After the caterpillar incident, I'm slumped on the grass. Tears are running down both cheeks. They meet on the point of my chin, hang there a while forming one big drop, and splash onto the pulverized caterpillar.

Thunder roars, and I look at the sky. Storm

clouds are forming. The gray clouds match the way I feel inside. I don't want to be different. I don't want to be a freak or a weirdo. I just want to fit in.

"Why can't I fit in? Oh!" I wipe my eyes and blow my nose on the bottom of my sweater vest. "I wish I fit in!" I sit there, tears still streaming down my face, while heavy fog surrounds me. But I don't care.

"What is 'fit in'?" Someone asks.

My eyes search to see who's talking to me but I'm not sitting on the edge of the playground anymore. I'm sitting on top of a hill in a flower-filled meadow with blue grass and green sky.

Wait a second! Blue grass and green sky?

"Where am I?"

I'm rubbing my eyelids with my fists, but the blue grass and green sky are still there when I open my eyes. Now I know I'm not on the edge of the playground. I'm someplace else. I'm someplace different! I start to panic.

"So, tell me, what is 'fit in'?" the person asks again.

I look down and there's a tiny girl about the size of a rabbit. The girl has wheels where her feet should be. She has a little bunny nose and big rabbity teeth.

I wipe away my tears on the back of my arm and answer her.

"It's being the same as everyone else so that you're not different."

"How boring!" The tiny girl shakes her head at me, clicks her big rabbity teeth, and rolls away down the meadow on her wheels.

CHAPTER FOUR: PLARBING

This is unreal. You know when you watch people in the movies pinch themselves to make sure what's happening isn't a dream? Well, this seems to call for something more. I must be dreaming, right? I haul off and punch myself in the nose as hard as I can.

"Argh!"

Nope. I clutch my throbbing nose. This is real. A trickle of blood drips onto my hand, and I swab it in the grass. My red blood on the blue grass turns the same shade of violet as the flowers on the playground. Now I'm standing up. This place is like nothing I've ever seen.

Okay. If you took all the crayons in a crayon box and dumped them out and mixed them around, not paying any attention to what should be colored what, then just randomly started coloring things whatever color of crayon you had in your hand. It's like that. It's a pretty place, but wow, it's different!

"Watch where you're plarbing, young lady!" I hear a man's deep voice say.

"Plarbing?"

Something hot and slimy rubs against me. Slime that smells half like cotton candy and half like the gunk that gathers in the kitchen sink drainer glops up my face and hair. I sneeze and can't tell if the goop hanging off the end of my nose belongs to me or...or the ginormous see-through gelatin man who's squishing against me!

The oozy goop slides to the end of my nose and just wriggles there a bit before plopping to the ground in a great big ball of jellied grossness. The gigantic, clear jelly man is shaped and moves like those giant garden slugs. Limax maximus. Not a fan.

"You are bipedal," he says, looking down at me, "and therefore might call it 'walking', the thing you do. To me it's 'plarbing'."

He-I guess it's he-sticks out his gloppy

tongue. It hangs there quivering. Another big ball of slime slowly rolls off onto the blue grass.

"I prefer to call your walking my plarbing," he says, spitting the rest of the slime in my direction. "It doesn't matter. It's all the same. You're in my way no matter what you want to call it."

He scoots himself past me and leaves a trail of slug-slime on every flower and every bit of grass he touches.

"I'm sorry," I call, but the enormous clear jelly man keeps sloshing along, paying no attention to me. I shudder and dab my nose on my sweater vest again. The humongous, oozing jelly guy slides along through the meadow and down the other side of the hill. He disappears into some trees.

When I'm sure he's gone, I walk-no, run! - toward the opposite edge of the meadow, making sure to watch where I'm stepping so I don't accidentally 'plarb' all over someone. Ahead is a pink cobblestone path bordered on one side by giant purple pickle trees.

CHAPTER FIVE: POINT OF VIEW

Yeah. I said pickle trees!

When I get to the start of the path, in the middle of all these pickle trees I spy a kiosk. You know, the kind of kiosk you see at the mall or at an amusement park with a map that shows *You Are Here* and maybe has some kind of public service announcement poster about parents needing to spend more time playing outside with their children before the kids grow up and leave the house for good.

I run up to it. It has a screen with a button to press for directions. I push the button and some canned music plays. The screen comes to life with a holographic image of a lady wearing pajamas, slippers, and those old-time squishy pink hair curlers. She stretches and yawns.

"Can I help you?" she asks in a tinny, robotic voice.

"Can you tell me where I am?" I ask.

Maybe this kiosk can tell me how to get back to Parkside Intermediate.

"This is Elsewhereville," says the hologram.

"Yes, but where is Elsewhereville?"

"It isn't anywhere and it isn't nowhere," the hologram in pj's says in the robotic voice.

"But it must be somewhere."

"No." The hologram shakes her head. "You're getting that confused with everywhere. Everywhere is somewhere."

Then the hologram disappears, and the screen goes dark. But before I have time to think, the screen lights up again, and the hologram woman stretches and yawns once more.

"This is Elsewhereville. It isn't anywhere and it isn't nowhere," it says.

"You've already told me..." I say, but she continues.

"No. You're getting that confused with everywhere. Everywhere is somewhere... This is Elsewhereville..."

I step away.

"You've *got* to be kidding me. This, right here, is why a fifth grader *needs* a cell phone."

I pick a pickle from one of the giant purple trees because I'm hungry and I'm pretty sure recess is over by now, and the kids are probably lining up for lunch, and because I'm pretty sure whoever planted these purple pickle trees won't mind if I grab just one pickle to eat.

I bite into my pickle and, oh my gosh, it tastes like lemon meringue pie! So, I hurry up and bite into it again, but this time it tastes gross! Kind of the way a truck's brakes smell when it's traveling down a really steep mountain. I spit that piece onto the ground, quick. For whatever reason, I take a third bite, and this time it just tastes like an ordinary dill pickle.

"You fancy our pickles?" Someone says.

"They're the best in the land."

Under one of the larger trees, I see a man balancing upside down on his head. He paints on a canvas with a really low easel. The man wears a long shirt like one of Grandma's tunics. It has paint splotches all over it like the old shirts we wear in art class when we're doing something messy. He has a big, flat hat. His hat is helping him keep his balance. His skin is the color of pencil lead (which is interestingly not lead at all, but graphite).

Now he waves his brush at me, so I walk over to this upside-down painter guy.

He's painting a picture of a beach scene on the canvas, but the picture is upside down, too, so the sky is the ocean, and the ocean is sky.

The painter turns his eyes up at me and smiles but then he frowns right away when he sees me.

"You have tears in your eyes. Why are you sad?" he asks.

Honestly, I kind of forgot all about the tears and the crying and the not fitting in until now.

"Because I'm different, I guess. I just wish I were...you know...normal like the other kids at school."

"Aw," the painter says. "Normal all depends on your point of view." He keeps painting. "What might seem normal to some people is different to others."

I turn my head upside down, too, to see what he sees. Now the ocean scene looks more like a herd of wild, blue horses running in the wind with their manes whipping back and forth. The painter dips his brush in a green bowl and then after stroking the canvas once, puts the brush in his mouth.

"Mmmm!" he says, licking the brush.

I think maybe this guy might be all fruit loops from standing on his head too long.

"It's pistachio pudding!" He smiles. He pulls out another brush from his tunic and dips this one into a different bowl of paint by his side. "Here," he says, handing me the brush and the bowl. "You can have it. It's tapioca."

"Thanks!" I say, dipping the brush in the bowl. "Can you tell me how to get to Parkside Intermediate School?"

"Never heard of it," the painter says. "But you are someone who will go far. So, I'm sure you'll end up in the right place." Then he goes back to painting his upside down or right-side-up canvas.

I walk down the pink cobblestone path dipping

the brush he gave me in my bowl and eating tapioca.

CHAPTER SIX: NEEP

I walk along the path for what seems like hours but when I look up again, there's the upside-down painter with the flat hat painting the same ocean scene or horses (whichever you prefer, depending on your point of view). I plop down in the grass with my bowl and search for some flowers or bugs to talk to.

The wind blows, and I swear it sounds like someone whispering the word "frrreeeeeaaaaakkkkkk," from overhead. I search the sky. There are two grimaces in the clouds, but when I stare harder, the clouds shift, and the grimaces disappear.

Pretty soon a normal-looking boy about my age zips past me down the path. He has short, black hair, and he's wearing neon green tennis shoes. I jump up and rush after this regular kid. Maybe he knows where Parkside Intermediate is and he's heading there now. I have to run to keep up with this guy. Where is he going in such a hurry?

We run next to a stream. There's a school of yodeling catfish! I kid you not. Nothing is surprising me now.

Their heads are out of the water and mouths wide open, singing. Their whiskers slap against the water every time they hit a high note. I cover my ears because the fish are horribly loud and horribly out of tune.

"You can't tune a fish," my dad would say. He's the king of corny jokes. I guess it's actually true this time.

The boy makes a sharp turn ahead and leaps over a little wooden bridge that crosses the stream. I jump, too, but I'm clumsy and I trip and fall headfirst into the water. I splash through the water and trudge up the muddy bank on the other side. I notice the boy has stopped running. Not only has he noticed me, but he's also waiting for me. I'm wringing out the bottom of my vest as I slosh myself up to him.

"Hello," I try to say, but I'm breathing so heavily from all of this that my hello just sounds like breathy little *Huh. Huh. Huhs.*

I hold out my wet hand in front of me to shake hands, but instead of shaking, this normal-looking boy just holds his hand to mine, fingers barely touching. Is he afraid of water? Maybe he doesn't want to catch any germs. I can respect that. I pull my hand back.

"Neep," he says.

"My name is Myrtle Hitchabocker," I say.

"Neep beep," says the boy.

"It's very good to meet you, Neep Beep. Can you tell me where the Parkside Intermediate School playground is?" I ask. "It's got to be around here somewhere."

My eyes search side to side.

"Neep beep. Beep beep meep neep," the boy answers.

"Umm..." I don't know what to say to this. Is he joking?

"Neep beep?" the boy says again. He shrugs

and frowns at me. Then he races off, green shoes kicking.

The boy zooms down the path. So much for normal-looking, I think. He's getting smaller and smaller. I can still see his neon green tennis shoes. Pretty soon I can't even see them anymore.

CHAPTER SEVEN: THREE CONFERRING CONIFERS

"Ew! She's not like us."

I turn around to see who said that, but there's no one there.

"Hello?"

"Don't talk to her!" someone says again, but all I can see along this portion of the path are a couple of Christmas trees with a sign in front of them that reads:

Three Conferring Conifers.

"What's a conferring conifer?" I wonder aloud. A conifer is a cone-bearing seed plant. Most of the conifers are trees, but some are shrubs. They belong to the division pinophyta. Trees like pine and cedar and cypress and spruce and redwood are all conifers.

And confer means to discuss. But conferring conifers? That doesn't make any sense.

"She's so weird-looking."

"Who said that?" I say. I weave around the trees searching for the culprit.

"Look at her leaves, the way they swirl around her top and her limbs stick out too far and her trunk's silly. It's all striped."

"Agreed! She's the ugliest Christmas tree I've ever seen."

"What?" I say, almost laughing. "Come on! Who are you? Where are you? Come out. Show yourself!"

"Her crown is messy, and her shape is all wrong."

I realize these three Christmas trees are the ones doing all the talking. Okay. This is the most bizarre thing so far. Where I come from, if you talk to flowers or insects, or even trees, they never talk back to you. This makes no sense.

The left tree says, "Where are her decorations? She doesn't have any decorations."

"You think I'm a Christmas tree, too, don't you?" I say.

"Oh yeah. What a pity for her. No decorations," says the tree on the right.

I stand there staring at them. "I'm right here, you know. I can hear everything you're saying. And by the way, I'm *not* a Christmas tree. I'm not even a regular tree."

On and on they talk about me like a couple of sixth grade gossips.

A breeze blows through the Christmas trees' branches, and pieces of limbs and pine needles stick in my hair. They tangle like when a hairbrush gets wound up in your hair. I try to get myself free as the trees continue to say nasty things to each other about me.

The tree on the left says, "Gross! Fuzzy animals are climbing up her trunk."

The tree on the right says, "I concur. She's gross!"

"Ew! Yeah!" The tree in the middle laughs.

Finally, I manage to untangle myself, but my hair is still bound, and a big clump of it pulls out and stays stuck around a branch.

"What is she doing?" asks the middle tree.

"It's like her trunk is splitting," says the tree on the right.

"Ewwwwww! And she's...she's moving!" the left Christmas tree says.

"Gross!" they all shout together.

I'm pretty annoyed by now and say, "I'm going to do something that the three of you can't. I'm going to walk away, and there's nothing you can do about it. Go ahead and call me names. I won't hear because I'm not going to hang around and listen."

"What is she doing?" the trees keep gossiping to each other. "Her roots are moving. She's moving! She's a freak! Ew! Gross! She's moving through the forest. What a weirdo."

You know what? As I move away from them, I can't hear the three stupid Christmas trees talking. But you know what else? They're just some silly trees, and anything they say can't hurt me.

I turn around and shout one more thing, "And furthermore, it's not even Christmas!"

CHAPTER EIGHT: RHINOCEROS

I saw a hippopotamus at the zoo once, but I've never seen a rhinoceros in real life. Those things are deadly. Not as deadly as hippopotamuses, mind you, but they can gore you out like a pumpkin for Halloween.

I've read that the average human can run about eight-point-three miles per hour, the fastest among us going as fast as fifteen-point-nine miles per hour. An average rhinoceros runs somewhere around thirty-one miles per hour. Say that I can run as fast as twelve miles per hour. That's a difference of nineteen miles per hour. Considering the rhinoceros is only about three hundred feet away, it would take the rhinoceros a much shorter amount of time to get to me than it would for me to sit down and finish calculating this rate/time/distance equation.

I'm thinking all these thoughts at one time. All the knowledge I have ever learned about rhinoceroses and hippopotamuses, and how deadly and fast certain animals are, comes flashing through my mind. I say all this because right at this very moment, a rhinoceros with an old-time open top carriage strapped behind it scrambles down the path towards me. A little driver sits on the coach box.

When the rhinoceros sees me, it whips its horn back and forth on the ground. It charges as fast as it can at me. It puffs and grunts, and dust flies under its powerful feet. The carriage jolts along behind it. The driver on the coach box is being tossed back and forth with no control.

I brace myself and close my eyes to prepare

to become the next gored out jack-o-lantern statistic. The rhino speeds closer and closer. I'm scrunching my eyes, holding my breath, clenching my fists, preparing to die...but nothing happens.

When I finally gather enough courage to open my eyes, the rhinoceros is standing in front of me. Its humungous face is just inches from my own. It breathes stinky rhinoceros' breath on me and lets out a sound like a deflating balloon. Then it licks my face with its sandpaper tongue.

The driver, a tiny, strangely dressed man with what looks to be a turnip for a nose, steps down from the carriage and stands next to me.

"My name is Border Wizzler," he says, holding his fist out for a fist bump. I bump fists with him but then he holds his fist out again. I bump it a second time. A third time he holds out his fist and I reluctantly bump it. Then he holds it out once more to fist bump. This could go on for days. I just wave at him and smile.

Border Wizzler's skin is the same pink color that shrimp turns when its boiled and cooked in a pot. The leaves on Border Wizzler's turnip nose are downturned above his lip just like a mustache. When he breathes, the leaf-mustache flies in and out of his mouth.

"Our town is Elsewhereville," he says, "You're welcome to stay in this fun land of ours until you've had your fill."

CHAPTER NINE: BORDER WIZZLER

"I don't mean to sound ungrateful, Mr. Wizzler," I say, "but for starters, I don't know how I got here. This is all too much. At one point I was sitting on the edge of the playground in the grass where the violets bloom at Parkside Intermediate School, thinking about how I don't fit in with the other kids and how they call me names like weirdo and freak, and now here I am talking to you in...in Elsewhereville."

My face grows hot, and my throat and stomach feel all bunched together inside. Tears form in my eyes and the waterworks start pouring again.

Border Wizzler blows his turnip nose and wipes his leaf mustache with a handkerchief. He pats me on the back.

"It's no one's fault you're not the same," he says. "It's just not right they call you a name. Because you are different? Well, that's just a shame. We all do different things. It's what makes us unique. Too bad that they call you a weirdo and freak."

Okay, I think to myself. Is this guy going to talk in rhyme the whole entire freakish time? Argh! Now I'm doing it. That makes the corners of my mouth turn up slightly, but I'm still crying.

Border Wizzler starts talking again. "Well, just

look at me. I only talk in rhyme. I really quite enjoy myself. I do it all the time."

The comparison of me bawling about how weird people think I am to a tiny guy with a turnip for a nose, who only speaks in rhyme, strikes me as hilarious, and I stop crying right away.

"I know what you can do!" he says to me, very serious, "You can fit in with us. If you're not exactly like we are, we promise we won't fuss."

"That's a gracious offer," I tell him, "But as much as I would *love* to stay here in Elsewhereville I'm sure my mom and dad will file a missing person report if I don't come home from school tonight."

I ask if he has a phone and Border digs around in the deep pockets of his oversized coat and hands one to me. The phone is shaped like a turtle shell and about as big as the palm of my hand. There's only a single button to press, no screen, and no numbers. I press the button over and over, but nothing happens. Then I hold it to my ear and wait. I stand there waiting another minute holding the turtle shell to my ear.

"With only one button and never a screen, our phones here are useless. You see what I mean?" he says, shrugging.

I hand back his phone.

"I've been the mayor here for an extra-long time. Was it before or after I started to rhyme?" he asks himself, stroking his leaf mustache.

In fact, he says he can't remember how long he has been the mayor because all the clocks in Elsewhereville run on fish scales, and it has been an awfully long while since anyone has bothered to change the fish scales in any of the clocks.

"Plus, all the calendars are made of mustard. It makes us all so very flustered."

He assures me it is quite difficult, if not next to impossible, to read mustard. I believe it!

He says, "For the days of the week instead of seven we have a few more. We have eleven. After Monday through Friday the weekend won't start. Four more days are tacked on, and that's not very smart. We've got Pingday and Podday, then there's Whimday and Wobday.

Eleven days in a week is way too confusing. We make each day Saturday. It's much more amusing."

"You mean you just treat every day like a Saturday?" I ask.

"Yes. Yes. That's right, I guess."

"Good thinking!" I say.

"No one in Elsewhereville knows the date, time or year. We can't call out to ask with our useless phones here."

I let him know it's Tuesday afternoon right after recess at Parkside Intermediate School.

CHAPTER TEN: THE CLOUD COUSINS AND A MOUNTAIN

Border Wizzler tells me his rhinoceros's name is Bill Worthington, but he likes to be called Fram. Right then, some big, dark angry clouds sweep across the green sky. They settle on the ground, still miles away but heading for us fast. The wind from the coming storm shakes all the pickles off the giant purple pickle trees and blows my hair into my eyes.

Bill Worthington, I mean Fram, whips his horn back and forth across the ground again.

Border Wizzler looks at me, and all the shrimp-pink color drains from his face. Even his turnip nose turns a pale white.

"The Cloud Cousins are coming. There's no time to gab. We've got to get moving. Quick! Hop in my cab."

Border Wizzler leaps up in the coach box and points behind him.

"Jump in the cab. Let's give it a whirl. I'm proud to be seen with such a nice girl."

I've never ridden in a carriage before, and as a general rule, I don't accept rides from strangers. But a rhinoceros-drawn carriage ride in the middle of an approaching storm in a place like this? Who's gonna turn *that* down?

I jump in the back, and Border jerks on the reins. Immediately, Fram races up the cobblestone path.

"Who or what are the Cloud Cousins?" I ask, but

Border and Fram are too busy concentrating on pulling ahead of the storm to answer my question.

I look behind me at faces in the clouds. I'm not talking about when you gaze at the clouds on a pretty day and use your imagination to spot a flying dragon carrying an Easter basket or maybe a cheetah wearing a sombrero. I'm talking two definite and for real faces in the clouds with eyebrows, glaring eyes, and sharp, biting teeth!

One of the cloud faces is wispy and long with tendril-like arms. It's reaching out for us and just a few feet behind the cab.

"Go faster, Fram!" I shout.

The other cloud has a puffy, angry face. This cloud fills its cheeks with air and blasts it on our little cab. The wind from its breath is snapping my hair across my head and whipping the back of my sweater vest against my back.

The Cloud Cousins with their huge, mean faces and reaching arms are right behind us. The long tendril arms flail like one of those inflatable air dancers at a used car lot. The air-dancer-arms look more like whips now, and their gust travels under my sweater vest and up my spine. My back and my ribs sting from the force of the wind. I swallow hard and mouth a prayer.

The two angry clouds circle the cab to block our way.

Suddenly, ahead on the path is the steepest mountain I've ever seen. Fram takes a running leap and dashes up the mountain.

I'm gripping the sides of the carriage as tight as I can to keep from rolling out and back down the mountain.

I dare to glance back. The Cloud Cousins are far behind, still at the foot of the mountain.

Up here the sky is its normal bright green (if green could ever be a normal color for a sky).

Border looks behind and lets out a happy "Whoop whoop!" His leaf mustache flaps in the wind. Then he says, "You never know where a mountain will be. That was a close one for you and for me. A mountain's waiting all the time to step in front or in behind. So always be prepared to climb!" He laughs at his own joke. "But just because a mountain steps in your way, that doesn't mean that you'll have a bad day. It's conversely the opposite. That's what I say!"

Border tells me the Cloud Cousins don't really like being clouds. They always wanted to be earthworms and so they are miserable and want everyone else to be too. I think that's sad.

Fram stops the carriage, and we teeter at the very top of the mountain with hardly enough room for both the carriage and Fram.

There's a valley at the foot of the mountain where I can make out a giant red X.

"Oh! This will be neat! Hold on to your seat!" Border says while trying on a ridiculously large pair of aviator goggles.

He reaches underneath his seat, pulls out another pair and hands them to me. Then he produces two flower pots, each with a single orange daisy growing out the top. He places his pot on his head and straps it under his chin. I see now it makes a pretty effective helmet.

I fit my flower pot on my head and slap the goggles over my eyes. Then I grip the seat just as Fram takes a flying leap off the edge of the mountain. We go careening down through the air.

I'm screaming! Border Wizzler's screaming! Fram's making that deflating balloon sound again! There's no doubt about it. We. Are. Going. To. Die!

CHAPTER ELEVEN: MELCOME TO ELSEWHEREVILLE

I say as many Hail Marys as I can possibly say in the span of thirty seconds.

Border cranks back on a big lever, and a parachute billows out over the carriage. We float to the ground right over top the giant red X.

"Don't you agree that that was fun? We could try it again now that it's done."

I just glare at Border as we remove our flower

pot helmets and goggles. I am not amused.

In front of us stands a road sign. Civilization. Familiarity. Normalcy.

The sign reads:

Melcome to Elsewhereville, where Different is Divine.

The W in 'Welcome' has been turned upside down, so it looks like an M. I can't tell if the sign maker wrote it that way on purpose or if someone came along and flipped the W.

Beyond the melcome sign is a town-at least I think it's a town. I've never seen one like it, but I'm learning to expect the unexpected here in Elsewhereville.

It's well past lunchtime as Fram pulls the carriage through town. The streets are filled with all kinds of excitement. There's a donut shop that sells creme-filled tires, and a tire shop that sells little black donuts.

Border stops the carriage in front of the tire shop. He hops out and buys a box of donuts for us to eat. He holds up the box to me in the carriage. I grab a donut in each hand, and so does Border.

The rest of the donuts go to Fram, who eats them in one gulp, box and all. I eat my two donuts almost as fast as Fram eats his. They're really good. I pick all the donut crumbs off my sweater vest and pop them in my mouth. We continue down the street with Fram hauling us in the carriage.

Some of the people here have antennas on their heads like my insect friends. Others have tails, spots, or stripes. Or tails, spots, *and* stripes. Some of the people are roaring like lions. Others whinny and neigh like horses. There's even a cow boy here. Not like a western cowboy with the hat and boots, an actual boy with a cow nose and ears and hooves. He moos at me when we pass him.

Some people have three legs or four arms. One lady even has a hand on the top of her head. She's holding a bag of popcorn with it as her right hand crams handfuls of popcorn into her mouth. She's pushing a baby stroller with her left hand. I think that third hand would really come in...handy. Oh brother! My dad would have a field day making up a bad joke about that.

There's a sound behind us like when you try to unclog the toilet with a plunger. It turns out to be a real cowboy (the western kind this time) riding a six-foot-tall grasshopper with suction cups for feet. The suction-cup feet make a *smuck!* sound each time the grasshopper pulls his feet up off the ground.

"Howdy, ma'am," the cowboy says, tipping his

hat at me.

"Hello," I say back.

The cowboy looks like a cowboy because he's wearing a cowboy hat and boots that the other cow boy was missing, but he's also wearing a big, pink tutu, so I imagine he must be some type of cowboy-ballerina.

Merriam-Webster defines the word 'eccentric' as "deviating from the conventional, especially in an odd or whimsical way." We are way beyond that here in Elsewhereville. Even the words 'weirdo' and 'freak' would have nothing on these people. They will have to come up with a whole new word to describe people from Elsewhereville.

I see now that the only thing the same about all the people here is that they're all different. Really different. And no one seems to care at all about fitting in. In fact, I'd say they would be pretty upset if they woke up one day and they were all just plain normal.

Right now, two houses go leapfrogging by. Okay...I know I said nothing is surprising me, but two whole houses playing a game of leapfrog *does* surprise me. I guess because they're just so big. I mean, they look like ordinary beach houses up on stilts, but when the houses raise their stilts to leapfrog over each other, it's like a couple of gigantic robotic hopping frogs.

A boy in one of the home's windows waves at me with both hands and I wave back.

CHAPTER TWELVE: GREETINGS AND SALUTATIONS!

"Greetings and salutations!" someone shouts.

I look in that direction, and there's only a doorpost with no house attached. The door swings out.

"Greetings and salutations!" a man (wearing a cat on his head) says. Then he slams the door shut. He swings it back open in a few seconds. "Greetings and salutations!" then he slams it shut again. A few more seconds pass and he's back at it with the greetings and salutations.

Border Wizzler stops the carriage, and the two of us get out. We walk up to the man at the doorpost, being careful to stay out of the path of the leapfrogging homes, of course.

Border points to the 'Greetings' guy. "This is Fred Flamminski. He wears a cat on his head," he says.

The orange tabby cat on Fred's head hisses at me, but Fred smiles an eager, gap-toothed smile, and we exchange waves.

"Greetings and salutations!" Fred shouts at me. Then he slams the door in my face.

"And tiny Willmina Persinsky." Border turns and points to a speck of a lady strolling past. "She's as thin as a needle and thread."

Three men walk down the street and stop in front of us. Border fist bumps them repeatedly. All the men take turns well-wishing, fist bumping, elbow bumping, and finally air pumping. They hold their hands over their hearts and pat each other on the back over and over. This goes on for several minutes and just as I start to search for some flowers or bugs to talk to, they stop.

"Old Philo McJonesmith," Border says to me, "where he should have a nose, instead of that he has five fingers and ten toes!"

Philo McJonesmith waves his nose fingers at me. I smile and wave back with my regular hand fingers.

"This is Nur LaNur from Nurdle Nur," Border goes on. "He talks out both sides of his mouth. But that's not a thing, cause every year Nur's brother grows wings and flies south!"

Right then Nur's brother, who has been standing next to us with Nur and Philo, sprouts big black wings and takes off flying through the sky.

Nur turns to me and says, "Good day!" with the voice from one side of his mouth, but his other voice from the opposite side sounds so much like a fork scraping against the side of a metal bowl that I want to slap my hands over my ears. But I don't dare because I don't want to look rude. Fortunately, he doesn't say any more.

"We really are all different and that is completely okay," Border says. "That's how we are made, and I say hooray! Hooray that we're all made that way!"

"You *are* all different here," I say, "It's nice. I like it."

CHAPTER THIRTEEN: TODD CROAKER

Nur and Philo walk with us down the street to a normal enough office building. There's a sign above the door that reads *Todd Croaker, Investment Broker*

in big, bold letters.

Border Wizzler steps up to the door and rings the doorbell. But instead of making a bell sound or even a buzz or some other electronic noise, the doorbell lets out a loud "ribbit-ribbit".

We all stand waiting outside the door listening to the ribbiting chorus play over and over till the door finally opens.

"Afternoon, Mayor!" croaks a man with bulging eyes and a massive double chin. His chin hangs out over his three-piece suit. His tie is tied so tight that I wonder if that's the reason the man looks a little green and his eyes poke out of their sockets.

"Are you ready to start the parade? It's your turn to marshal today. The last time you tried to evade, so, this time you won't get away," Border Wizzler says impatiently.

"Now, Mayor..." the man says, then he sees me and grabs my hand with his webby fingers.

"Todd Croaker, Investment Broker," he says to me, jerking my arm up and down in a violent handshake. He manages to slip a business card into my palm. I read it:

"Todd Croaker, Investment Broker.

When you need a broker, remember Todd Croaker

for all your investment needs."

"Myrtle Hitchabocker," I say. "But I don't have any money to invest."

"Money?" He laughs. "Why would someone invest in something as risky as money?" He laughs some more. "I help people invest in themselves. Money! Bah!"

As he speaks, he takes a tin out of his breast pocket. He opens the tin of what looks like breath mints, but I see right away that they're dead flies. He hands the open tin to me to take one, but I politely shake my head *no* and hand it back. I couldn't bear the thought that I might be eating a distant relative of one of my insect friends back on the playground at school.

Todd Croaker's long, skinny tongue strikes out and laps up one of the flies, then he shuts the tin and tucks it back in his pocket.

"Perhaps, Myrtle Hitchabocker," Todd Croaker says, "you'd do me the great honor of sharing with me the title of grand marshal for today's parade?"

"Yes!"

"Good-oh!" he says. "You've already started investing."

CHAPTER FOURTEEN: THE EVERYDAY PARADE

"Bedlam, hullabaloo and pandemonium!" Todd Croaker shouts. "It's time for the Everyday Parade."

The whole street stops what they're doing, and everyone joins in the Everyday Parade.

"You'll like this," Todd says to me. "The Everyday Parade celebrates what makes everyone different. We celebrate it every day, so we don't forget how important it is to be unique."

Border hands Todd Croaker and me each a baton, and we line up at the front of the parade. Border, Nur, and Philo fall in line behind us.

A man in Border's row has a large grape jelly stain on his striped sweater vest. He points from his vest to mine. "Hey! Hey! Look at us!" he says beaming with pride.

That makes me laugh. Then I'm laughing some more. Then I'm positively bursting and bending over in a full fit of laughing.

Border pats me on the back, "You know that when a laugh begins its usually better out than in."

This reminds me of something corny that my dad would say about a fart and that makes me laugh even harder.

Music blares, and I see four musicians in the back row. The first has a trumpet that is sticking out of his face in the place where his mouth and nose should be. He blasts his trumpet-nose-mouth with all his might, and it lets out a brassy *Zert! Zert!*

The next musician is a curvaceous woman wearing a crop top. She has a tiny waist with the biggest belly button ever. It's just a huge hole in the middle of her stomach. She's strumming five strings that run across her empty stomach hole with her long pointy fingertips and this makes a *Plink! Plink!* sound.

The third player is as round as he is tall. He has a wide, white face that he beats with drumsticks in a *rap, tap, tap* cadence. His eyes blink shut, and his mouth puckers up with each tap.

The last player just boings himself loudly on the head with a big percussion mallet in perfect rhythm with the other musicians. *Boing! Boing! Boing!*

As far as appearances, this is the most unorganized parade I've ever been to. Everyone is out of step. Some people are almost running as they march. Others have barely moved since the parade started. A couple of people marched backwards, someone is marching in circles, and one guy marched himself sideways, right into an alleyway. Several people have tripped over each other, and no one is worried about being in step with anyone else. But each person seems to have their place in this parade. Yeah. It's the most disorganized parade I've ever been to, but also the most fun.

Something tugs at my sock.

"Hello again!" It's the little girl with big, rabbity teeth and wheels for feet, the girl I met in the meadow when I first got here.

"Hello!" I say, happy to recognize her.

"'Fitting out' is way more fun than 'fitting in', isn't it?" the rabbity girl shouts up to me.

"It certainly is!" I say.

CHAPTER FIFTEEN: CIRRUS AND CUMULUS

The green sky is turning from a pretty pea-green to a deep emerald.

Todd Croaker points his baton up to the sky. "Uh-oh!" he croaks, "It's the Cloud Cousins, Cirrus and Cumulus."

"Oh no!" I say. "We ran into them earlier on the

road here."

"Don't worry about them, Myrtle," Todd says. "They like to blow through here from time to time and try to rain on our parade. They're just a lot of wind. They can't really hurt you if you remember that."

He gives me a reassuring smile. "Even still," he says, "Let's get out of their path."

He grabs my baton and hops out of the way down a long alley. Then he waves for me to follow.

The parade-goers dart back and forth across the street trying to seek shelter. I'm almost to the alley with Todd when the Cloud Cousins make a straight shot for me. The big, fluffy one, who I assume must be Cumulus because of her shape, fills her bloated cheeks and directs all her air at me. I stumble backward and lose sight of Todd Croaker.

The other thin-shaped cousin must be Cirrus. She rocks me from side to side with her wispy tendrils as Cumulus comes huffing and puffing up into my face. She blasts all her wind on me.

"Thought you could get away from us, huh?" she bellows.

Cumulus and Cirrus take turns blowing me back and forth between them. The motion whirls me around and around. Cumulus's enormous cheeks fill with air and blow me faster so I'm spinning like a top.

"I'm gonna puke!" I scream.

I stop spinning but I'm still being pushed between the two of them.

"I'm sorry you feel bad about not being earthworms and all, but this has nothing to do with me...I can weather this storm!" I shout.

"What did you say?" asks Cirrus.

I shout, "I said I can weather this storm."

"No. Before that...Let her go, Cumulus. She's right," says Cirrus, but the wind they've created is so strong it shoves me down the street and I don't see them again.

A pygmy goat on a tricycle goes sailing past me, bleating and backpedaling.

I catch sight of Border Wizzler. He's clutching tight to a flagpole with his feet off the ground. His turnip leaf mustache is flapping up into his eyes. I look around for Todd Croaker, but he's nowhere in sight.

Border Wizzler is saying something to me now, but I can't make out what he's saying over the howling wind. I'm losing my footing and sliding down the street.

"What did you say?" I yell to him.

"It's okay to be you," he shouts, ""Because that's what you do!"

I'm picking up speed, rolling away and can barely see Border now.

"If you were me, what fun would that be?" he cries over the gale.

Everything is suddenly fog. I've stopped rolling and sit there for a few seconds. The wind is gone, and it's peaceful and quiet. When I rise, the fog is so thick I can't even see where it ends and where my body starts.

CHAPTER SIXTEEN: BACK AT PARKSIDE

"Hey, freak show!"

It's Sierra Simpkins.

No doubt about it, I'm back on the edge of the playground where the violets grow.

The fog disappears, and Sierra's right in my face. "You been gone so long we all thought you ran away and joined the other freaks at the circus."

I laugh and pat her on the back the way a parent or teacher would when they think you've said something dumb, but they don't want to call you on it.

"Actually," I say, "it wasn't a circus. It was a parade."

She stands there for a while glaring at my hand still on her shoulder. She finally spouts, "You weirdo!"

That's all she can think to say, I guess.

Mrs. MacDugan, my fifth period English teacher, comes running up behind her. Sierra takes off at the sight of a teacher.

"There you are, Myrtle," Mrs. MacDugan says. "Everyone was looking for you. Recess is over. It's time for class, and we have a new student I'd like you to meet."

Standing beside her is a boy with black hair and neon green tennis shoes.

"Myrtle, this is Neep. His family just moved here, and I thought maybe you could show him around and help him with things until his English improves?"

After recess, I found out that a lot of things are still the same as before. I still have to wear Ethyl Mae's old clothes. The kids still call me names like 'weirdo' and 'freak'. My family's still poor. The Simpkins Sisters still laugh at me and make faces. But I feel better about myself now. I've learned that fitting out is okay. I'm okay with being different. Being me. And, oh yeah, I've made a new friend. A new boy in my class... A very normal-looking boy.

"Hello! I'm Myrtle Hitchabocker," I say.

"Neep Beep!" says the boy.

ABOUT THE AUTHOR

Melanie J. Vogel loves writing books for kids with BIG imaginations. An expert in the art of daydreaming and counting clouds, she lives in Cumberland, Maryland, and is a momma to one grown daughter. Happily married, she's a poodle lover, master flower gardener, and a casual unicorn spotter. Join her on Facebook at www.facebook.com/melaniejvogel.author and on her website at www.melaniejvogel.com.

If you've enjoyed reading ELSEWHEREVILLE, please consider writing a brief review at the site where you purchased it or on Goodreads.com.

Made in the USA
Middletown, DE
09 March 2022